RED BANTAM

RED BANTAM

by Louise Fatio, illustrated by Roger Duvoisin

McGraw-Hill Book Company New York · Toronto · London · Sydney

Library of Congress Catalog Card Number: 62-19760

ISBN 07-020058-0
67890 HDEC 754321

Red Bantam was the smallest
of all the animals on Monsieur Dumollet's farm.
That is, except Michel the canary.
Mother Hen knew all along he would never be big and strong,
for his egg was the smallest in the nest.
Indeed, it was a Bantam egg.
Madame Dumollet had slipped it among the big brown eggs
because she loved Bantams. They were so pretty and clever.

"Imagine my laying a Bantam egg,"
said fat Mother Hen, very much pained.
"And what a wee Bantam it is too."

Not even bothering to find a real name for him,
she just called him Bantam.
And when bright red feathers began to grow all over the chick
everyone called him RED BANTAM.

Now the chick from the biggest brown egg
grew so tall and strong and strutted with such swagger
he was called BIG ROOSTER.

Big Rooster looked handsome as he sang out
from the top of the wall at the entrance to the farmyard,
"Cocoricooo, look-at-me-and-see-what-a-fine-rooster-I-am."
"Oui, vraiment," said Monsieur Dumollet to his wife,
"I never saw a finer rooster."

Red Bantam, who overheard, thought sadly,
"No one could ever say such nice things about me.
Monsieur Dumollet even said the other day that
my cocoricos were like the shrieks from a broken clarinet."

Red Bantam never finished a whole cocorico.

As soon as he began one,

Big Rooster broke it off and chased him out of the yard.

"How dare you sing in my farmyard," shouted Big Rooster.

"Run away from my sight, you scraggly little creature."

Poor Red Bantam never dared to come close to the hens.
When he tried, Big Rooster came dancing on his long legs,
puffing his feathers to look bigger, and shoved him away.
"Cocorico," sang Big Rooster. "I am the master of this farmyard.
Who would dare say otherwise?"

Red Bantam was all the more unhappy
because among the hens there was Nanette—
Nanette the lovely hen with a plumage like a partridge's.
How dainty she was. Red Bantam loved her very much,
but how could he tell her under Big Rooster's ever-watching eyes?

So, Red Bantam spent his days at the duck pond behind the stable.

This was a lonely place for a rooster,

for the ducks stayed mostly in the middle of the pond,

or waddled in the thick mud around its edge.

But Jules the duck liked Red Bantam, and he said to him,

"You are nimble and clever. Why don't you stand up to Big Rooster

instead of hiding out here with that sad, beaten look?"

"Stand up to Big Rooster?" exclaimed Red Bantam astonished.

"Big Rooster the master of our farmyard?"

"Who said he was the master?" protested Marguerite the cow.

"He said so himself," said Marcel the pig.

"If you ask me, Big Rooster is but a fat bully."

"He is so big and I am so small and weak," sighed Red Bantam.
"I know there is no place for me in Big Rooster's farmyard."

Monsieur Dumollet thought so too, and he said to his wife,
"We can't keep your rooster on our farm. *Ça ne va pas.*"
"*Comme c'est dommage,*" said Madame Dumollet. "Look,
he is like a little prince dressed for a dance;
he walks so much more prettily than your swaggering Big Rooster."
"*Ma chère,* he couldn't even protect our hens against sparrows,
and in a rooster boldness is what counts. Tomorrow is market day,
I'll go to the village and sell him."

17

But early the next morning, while the farmer slept,
a great commotion fell upon the farmyard.
It all began when a blue jay swooped down from a tree, crying,
"Watch out, watch out! Everybody run. The Fox! The Fox!"
The ducks dove into the pond,
and all the chickens and Big Rooster too,
scattered in every direction, screaming in fright.
All ran except Nanette, who was shrieking in the hedge by the pond,
where the fox had caught her by the tail.

And except Red Bantam, who, seeing Big Rooster run for cover,
shouted his first real cocorico
and fell furiously upon the fox to save Nanette.
He fought with his claws, his spurs, his bill, his fast wings.
He struck the fox's nose, his ears, his back, his eyes.

He was a screaming, angry ball of feathers

flying circles around his enemy.

So fast was he, he made the fox turn upon himself like a top.

The fox had let Nanette go, but was choking on her tail feathers.

He was blinded by Red Bantam's flying thrust,

and deafened by his cries.

Hardly knowing where he was, he fell into the pond with a splash

among the "quack, quack, quack," of the frightened ducks.

"Cocoricooo," sang Red Bantam while the fox swam out of the pond

and ran, dripping wet, to hide his shame in the wood.

Monsieur and Madame Dumollet,
stumbling up from their bed to the window,
understood at once what had happened.
There, in the middle of the yard, Red Bantam was singing,
his feathers ruffled and bloody, his chest swollen with pride,
while, far away, the fox was slinking into the wood.
"Cocoricoooo," sang Red Bantam,
"it is *I,* the guardian of the farmyard.
Let all the foxes in the woods know, and Big Rooster too.
Cocoricoooo . . . ooooo."

"Ah, alors," said Madame Dumollet, "it's the brightest cocorico
I have ever heard. You see how brave is my little Bantam?"
"Ça c'est vrai," said her husband. "We mustn't sell him."

Nanette, who still looked pretty without a tail,
came out of hiding to thank Red Bantam.
"You were so courageous and clever," she said shyly.

Red Bantam made a little dance for her
and placed some grains of corn in front of her,
which is a rooster's way of saying, "I love you."

Then, one by one the hens came back to flock around him.

"To think I never saw how handsome he was," said one.

"His neck feathers are the color of ripe wheat,

and his comb is like the wild, red poppies."

"And his voice," said another, "is as beautiful

as the soldiers' trumpets on the fourteenth of July."

But who was slowly coming in now? It was Big Rooster.

Not the blustering Big Rooster, but a silent one,

who stood by himself in a corner of the farmyard.

Red Bantam went up to him and said,
"Big Rooster, let's be friends. You see, if we aren't,
Monsieur Dumollet will sell you on market day.
And, after all, I will share the farmyard with you."

What could Big Rooster do when he saw very well
that to be big, to sing loud, and puff out one's feathers,
do not make one a true rooster after all?
He embraced Red Bantam, and they both swore
they would be true friends for ever and ever.

"Bravo," cried Madame Dumollet. "Now, Monsieur Dumollet,
you can have your Big Rooster and I my beautiful Red Bantam.
And no fox will ever dare risk a bath in the pond."
From that day there was peace and love on Monsieur Dumollet's farm.

JP   Cop.9
                                      (EXT)

Fatio
  Red Bantam